◈   ◈

Words of color, words of song
Stories that bind the threads together
and hold the sun strong in its place
Flame in the darkness
Shine your thin, sweet voice
and we'll light the world
with one small kindness.

LIGHT

Stories of a Small Kindness

◈Nancy White Carlstrom◈

Illustrated by Lisa Desimini

Little, Brown and Company
Boston   Toronto   London

For Betty Celís de Jimenez of Mérida, Mexico, and
Sister Joan Margaret of Port-au-Prince, Haiti — your
lives are as light, bright kindnesses many
NWC

For Maureen — a bright, kind friend
LD

First Edition

Royalties from this book will benefit CTDUCA —
a school for children with Down's syndrome in
Mérida, Mexico — and Saint Vincent's School
for Handicapped Children in Port-au-Prince, Haiti.

Library of Congress Cataloging-in-Publication Data

Carlstrom, Nancy White.
    Light: stories of a small kindness/by Nancy White Carlstrom;
illustrated by Lisa Desimini. — 1st ed.
        p.   cm.
    Summary: A collection of seven short stories reflecting places as
diverse as Mexico, Haiti, New York City, and Guatemala.
    ISBN 0-316-12857-0
    1. Children's stories, American.   [1. Short stories.]   I. Title.
PZ7.C2184Li 1990
[Fic] — dc20   90-6552

10 9 8 7 6 5 4 3 2 1
BP

Published simultaneously in Canada
by Little, Brown & Company (Canada) Limited

Printed in the United States of America

◈ ◈

Contents

Song of the Cave

Manuel edged his way down into the hidden entrance and moved carefully into the cool darkness of the cave. As he did, he thought of the first time he had walked into the Hotel Maya. It was the only place in town with air conditioning. Not that it always worked. But he remembered how strange his skin had felt as he passed from the heat of the noonday sun into that cool hotel lobby. He had only been there, at the hotel, to deliver a pair of sandals Grandfather had made for one of the guests. I'll be here in this cave much longer, he thought to himself.

Grandfather had told Manuel stories about the cave — *la cueva*. Not many in their Yucatán village even remembered that it was there, hidden so well below the jagged edges of rock and yucca. Manuel had never mentioned the cave while playing with his friends in the schoolyard. He wanted it to be his secret, even though he had not been inside. Until today.

Manuel shivered. His eyes were getting used to the darkness. As he moved the candle higher in front of him, he was surprised at how much he could see.

Coming here was his own idea, and Manuel's ten-year-old body stood up taller with the thought. He would guide *turistas* to the cave. They would pay him big tips, money that would help his family. It sounded easy; at least it did when he was standing in the bright sunlight.

"It's okay if your candle goes out once," Grandfather had said when Manuel first talked to him about taking *turistas* to the cave. "That will give them a small scare. They will remember visiting *la cueva* and will tell their friends to go too. And they will be grateful to you, Manuel, when you relight the candle. It will mean a bigger tip, my grandson. But you must show no fear of the cave or the darkness," the old man muttered. "That would be bad. Bad for business."

Manuel had nodded in agreement, but something deep within him stirred.

So now Manuel was here in the cool cave to practice. He needed to find his way around. Alone. If he could manage being in the cave alone, then he could be a guide.

The cave was much bigger than Manuel had imagined. And quiet. Manuel missed the low grumble of the skinny turkeys that endlessly strutted through his yard and the rumble of the tour bus that stopped at Margarita's store.

Manuel sometimes leaned low on the whitewashed

stone wall in front of his house and watched *los turistas*. They were on their way to the ruins, but got out across the road to walk around and buy cold bottles of soda.

Manuel's sister Ana sold sweet buns and bars of chocolate from a tray that hung by a strap around her shoulders. Mostly the tourists bought the bars of chocolate. "Because they're wrapped in paper," Mamá said. If only they knew how long the bars had been sitting on the dusty shelf in back of Margarita's. They should buy Mamá's sweet buns, hot and sticky fresh every morning.

Now Manuel realized it was not silent in the cave. There was a small fluttering noise. Birds, perhaps? Manuel walked cautiously toward the sound. His sandals, the ones Grandfather made from old tires, kicked up small stones. One pebble lodged under his big toe and Manuel knelt to take it out.

"Take them to the big room, Manuel. You must do that," Grandfather had told him. "Pieces of broken pottery sit in the front. *Los turistas* will think it's an old Mayan altar."

Manuel stood up and followed the path. It did smell old in here, very old. He wondered if his Mayan ancestors had used *la cueva*. And if so, for what?

Suddenly the narrow tunnel opened up into the wide room. The ceiling was high and the space seemed even larger than it was. The circle of light from Manuel's candle was getting smaller.

I am getting smaller too, thought Manuel, and he did not feel nearly as brave as when he first entered the cave.

Something seemed to push against him, even in all this space. He put down his candle and brushed off both arms.

Were the old spirits hovering over him? What did they do in this place anyway?

He must remember to ask Grandfather. *Los turistas* would want to know.

Manuel picked up the candle and walked to the front of the room, where the pottery pieces sat. But as he did, a gust of wind whooshed over him. The candle went out without a flicker. Bumps of fear stood up on his arms and he tried to shake his head free from the ringing in his ears.

Manuel fumbled in his pocket for the matches. It was a new box he had taken from the cooking house. Mamá would need them for the evening supper soon.

But there was nothing. Nothing in his pocket. The matches were gone and Manuel fingered the torn threads of a pocket hole. How could it be? This was not part of his plan and certainly not the way of a guide. First, he felt disappointment sitting strong in his throat. Then he felt the fear again. No matches. No light. And darkness blacker than Manuel had ever seen before, yet strangely familiar.

Manuel turned to start back toward the tunnel. But then, there was the flapping of wings again. It startled him and he jerked around toward the sound. Even as he did, he knew he should not have. Now he had lost his sense of direction. Which way was back? Which way was the tunnel that would lead him to the cave's entrance?

With hands outstretched, he edged forward. At last he touched the cool rocks that formed the outer wall of the room. Slowly, his hands led him around it.

Time passed, but Manuel could not say how much. His stomach was growling; perhaps his family was eating tortillas and black-bean soup at this very moment.

He sat down and leaned against the wall to rest, but not for long. Or had he fallen asleep? It was hard to tell in the darkness. It seemed as if life had stopped for him.

I am going to be sick, thought Manuel. And then he remembered the time he had had the fever, as a small boy. His nights were hot and sweaty as he tossed through nightmares. There was darkness then. Yes, like this. The kind that seemed to swallow him.

He had kicked and fought against it. And he had almost lost. But then his mother held him in her arms and rocked him and sang to him in her weary voice. Her small song grew and grew and became a light for him to follow out of the darkness.

Manuel remembered all this, as he tried to clear himself of the nausea that gripped him. He heard the flapping of wings again, this time directly over his head. And he heard the words of that song, "El Rorro" — Rocking the Child. *A la rururu, chiquito querido, Duérmase ya mi Manuelito . . .* "*A la rururu,* ah baby, dear one, Oh little Manuel, sleep,

◈ 5 ◈

my son." Manuel smiled as he thought of his mother singing his name in place of the Christ Child's.

The sound of the birds grew fainter now, as if they were flying high and free. And then a tiny hope filled Manuel's mind with its own bright light. Maybe there was another way out of the cave.

Manuel felt his way along gingerly, as the ground sloped upward. He slipped on loose dirt and grabbed at the darkness, knicking his hands against a sharp rock. He knew his knuckles were bleeding, but still he climbed. He climbed toward the song and the air and the flapping of wings.

He climbed out of the dark, dank cave into the night. The stars were out and Manuel looked up at them, as if for the first time. He breathed in the fresh air and his whole body shook. Two swallows swooped over his head, and then flew off, leaving him in silent peace.

◈　◈　◈

On the way home, Manuel stopped at the church. He knelt before the Holy Mother and Child. Giving thanks, Manuel lighted his candle, the candle of the cave, and left it there.

Outside, an old woman wrapped in a shawl against the night air motioned for Manuel to stop. At first, he thought she wanted to sell him one of the religious pictures she kept in a bag by the church door.

He started to turn away, but her hand reached out and

pressed two objects into his. He walked as far as a street-light and held them up to see.

A box of matches. His own mother's box of kitchen matches! Of this, he was sure. And a new candle. Manuel stood wise-grown and ready to go home. Tomorrow he would return to the cave and would not be afraid.

Miracles of Isabela

After the news had traveled through the village of Santo Domingo — up the one cobbled street where the tiny market stalls leaned against one another and down the winding path to the central plaza — people shook their heads and wondered. Why had Doña Paloma done such a foolish thing in the first place?

But then, not many in this village of southern Mexico understood her anyway. Why would someone as educated as the Doña spend all her time and money on such a helpless group of *niños* — children who smiled and shuffled along but could not answer a simple question when asked?

They said some came from as far away as the capital to live at Doña Paloma's big house. And she was teaching them. *¡Increíble!* Tongues clicked in amazement at such an idea.

◈ ◈ ◈

It all started on a Wednesday, when Doña Paloma read

on the notice board near the church that a nativity play would be performed the following Sunday in Santiago. Even as she reread the notice, she was trying to figure out how to take the children on such a long trip.

By Thursday, Doña Paloma had convinced Pedro García to drive them to Santiago in his ancient school bus. Actually, it had been a school bus in its former life in the United States; now, Pedro used it to carry tourists around. Isabela, as Pedro fondly called the tired but dependable vehicle, knew her way over the mountain roads almost by herself. Most certainly she could get them to Santiago.

Doña Paloma bustled around on Friday and Saturday getting everything ready for the twelve children. Tía Luisa, a woman who helped in the house, would also accompany them. She, like the old bus, could not conceal her many years of service.

Sunday morning early, before the bells of Santo Domingo rang in the day, Isabela coughed her way off into the first gray light of dawn.

Doña Paloma sat on the seat behind Pedro García. As they left the sleeping village behind, she leaned over to inquire about the health of his family. Then Doña Paloma stood up and went back to be with the children. Pedro flipped on his tape player. It was not until he had to turn the tape over that he noticed the quiet.

These children do not talk much, he thought.

The observation startled him, as his own Elena and

Miguel chattered constantly. At this very moment, he realized the trip was not an ordinary one. Pedro tingled with an excitement he would later describe as fear.

The road twisted and curved up the mountainside. The children had trouble sitting upright in their seats, as the bus swerved and lurched over bumps. Isabela chugged and spluttered up the steep incline, while Pedro coaxed her along gently with the promise of an easy ride down.

At the top, they left the dust behind. Gray sheets of rain slanted against the mountain, and now mud pulled at the tires as they descended into the valley.

About halfway down, Pedro squinted his eyes. What was that below? A roadblock? An accident? He reached over and turned off the tape player, then tightened his hands on the steering wheel. He cleared his throat nervously.

Little pieces of a song floated up from the back of the bus. Doña Paloma was singing to the children. Pedro could not catch all of the words, but it was something about a sparrow singing "God comes to earth this day, Amid the angels flying."

Like little birds, some of the children twittered along in short, unrecognizable phrases. All swayed in their seats to the rhythm, completely unaware of their driver's apprehension. Pedro could see more clearly now. There were five men and he could sense danger in the way they waited, pacing back and forth in the middle of the road.

Pedro's heart thumped loudly in his chest and all he

could think of was *el sopilote,* the big, black vulture that swooped down to feast on carrion. He shivered at the thought.

Pedro slammed his foot onto the brake pedal and Isabela slid to a stop. The man who motioned to him had a gun. "*¡Bandidos!* Dear Mother of God," Pedro whispered. "Twelve helpless children, an old woman, Doña Paloma singing about a sparrow, and poor Pedro García. Isabela pray for us."

The man with the gun shouted for everyone to get off the bus. He looked so sure of himself — until the children came out, smiling into the rain. Each child looked up as if the man had just announced a fiesta. Now he looked confused and went to talk with the others.

The men talked, then argued. As the shouts grew louder, Pedro feared they would all be shot. He could imagine his wife sobbing, his children with sad eyes.

But Doña Paloma was getting out the sandwiches and bottles of juice from the bulging bag — *la bolsa* — she carried off the bus. Several of the older children balanced food carefully in their hands and with great concentration moved slowly toward the men.

Pedro watched the strange procession. The children walked like kings bearing great gifts to these dirty, unshaven men just out of hiding in the hills.

Suddenly, the man with the gun broke the silence. He ordered everyone back on the bus. "We all go together," he said. This will be a long ride, thought Pedro, as he pulled the door shut.

The children got settled again in their seats, then continued to eat their lunches and smile. Pedro saw one man reach over to hold the juice bottle for the smallest child, Benito, who was struggling to drink through a straw. Benito grinned shyly at him and started to speak, but no words came. This was not unusual, since no words had ever come before.

Five kilometers outside of Santiago, the leader told Pedro to stop the bus. The men got up. As they passed down the aisle, Benito's tiny voice chirped for the first time in his life, "*Dios le bendiga*" — God bless you.

◈   ◈   ◈

Pedro had not planned to attend the pageant. He intended to find a café and sip a hot drink or sit on the bench in the plaza and read the newspaper. But now, well, things were different now.

As he settled himself into a seat behind Doña Paloma and the children, next to wheezing Tía Luisa, he leaned over to the Doña and said, "I have seen one miracle today. Maybe there will be a second."

Doña Paloma nodded and, smiling, said, "But Pedro, there have already been two."

Skybird to the High Heavens

My name is Rosa. Rosa Lucas Paíz. I once lived in a land where footbridges dangled high above rushing streams and mountains stretched up green to the sky. Somehow the cows kept from falling off the steep cliffs.

"Grandmother, who keeps the cows in place?" I asked when I was a young girl.

"The same one who keeps the sun in the sky," my grandmother answered as she sat weaving on the floor of our house.

Corn grew in my land. Corn grew in patches on the side of the mountains where the cows did not fall. Grandmother said corn was one of the most important things we had. Corn gave us life.

My grandmother taught me how to weave. She had pieces of old weavings her grandmother gave to her when she was a girl. One day, she took them out and showed me.

"Rosa, these are the designs of our people." And she explained to me how each village used certain colors and designs in the weaving of cloth.

"I have saved these samples for many years, so I could pass them on to you. When I die, you will have them to use as patterns, so our own special weaving will live on."

As Grandmother taught me to weave, she told me stories about our land and its living things.

"Grandmother, tell me again about the time you saw the quetzal."

And Grandmother told me yet another time about when she was a girl and traveled far to the lowlands with her family. There, as they passed through the jungle, Grandmother had glimpsed the most beautiful bird in the world. The quetzal had blue-green tail feathers that stretched out three feet long. On its head was a tuft of gold and its chest wore a blood-red vest.

"If only I could see a quetzal someday, Grandmother."

"Maybe you will, my child. Maybe you will."

That night, I dreamed I rode on the back of a quetzal. I felt the rush of the wind as we soared to the high heavens. In the morning, I told my grandmother about my dream.

"How could I ride a quetzal, Grandmother?" I asked. "Did the bird become large, or did I become small?"

"Perhaps the dream was telling you that soon you must become small and hide from the danger wandering through

our land. No matter what happens, may you always remember the sweet smell of the earth, my child."

I knew my grandmother was talking about the war that was tearing our country apart, like a hideous beast. But still, I did not fully understand her warning.

And so, all morning as I did my chores, I daydreamed about becoming small. Small enough to hide behind the clay cooking pots my mother kept by the fire. Maybe if I jumped out I could surprise her and make her laugh.

I could be small enough to hide in an ear of corn and watch the sun glow on my father's back as he lifted the hoe.

"Father, why do you spend so many hours weeding the corn?" I asked, when he came home with rough hands and a tired back.

"Why, Rosa, if I allow the weeds to grow, the souls of the corn plants will move to cleaner fields. Then what would we eat, my daughter? How could we trade to buy the tools we need, the sandals you wear on your feet?"

"Sell the stories Grandmother tells as she weaves on her loom," I said with a laugh.

Father just shook his head, but Grandmother smiled to herself and I knew she would tell me another tale later, when the crickets sang.

That night, Grandmother told me of the great earthquake that leveled our village before I was born. She told me how the houses folded like paper and how giant rocks were tossed from the mountains like pebbles. It was a sad, true story.

"We thought the sun would fall from the sky that time. But it didn't, Rosa," she said quietly.

"Grandmother, when you saw the quetzal in the jungle, did you want to catch him and bring him home?"

"No, Rosa, I knew the quetzal was a bird of freedom. A cage would kill him. There are other ways to enjoy his beauty."

That night, my dreams were troubled. I could not ride the quetzal to the high heavens. I could not hide behind my mother's cooking pots or in the corn of my father's field.

"Where will I go?" I cried. "Where will I go?"

In the morning, soldiers came and burned our village. First, I hid. Then, as the whole sky turned black, I ran and ran. I could not look back.

◆   ◆   ◆

My name is Rosa. Rosa Lucas Paíz. I now live in a place far from where the footbridges dangle above the rushing streams and the mountains stretch green into the sky.

"Grandmother," I whisper, "the cows have fallen off the cliff. The sun has dropped from the heavens and the corn rots."

I miss the corn that gave me life. I miss the pot of water my mother kept boiling all day on the fire. I miss the hoe of my father chopping in time with our people for hundreds of years. I miss the stories my grandmother told and the threads of color she wove on the loom.

"Grandmother," I whisper, "what if I forget the sweet smell of the earth? What if they put all the quetzals into cages?"

This morning, as I walk to the place where I work in the refugee camp, I am surprised to hear someone call my name.

"Rosa." The voice is thin, like burnt paper, almost ready to crumble into little pieces.

"Rosa."

It comes to me across the miles that I have traveled while running in the cold night and burning day — fleeing through the cornfields, meeting up with others from distant villages, living pressed up close, finding shelter together from the winter rains. I see again a shared blanket, a cup of water and warm tortillas passed around, and these are like sparks of light in the darkness of my memories.

"Rosa, Rosa, is that you, dear?"

And there before me is a shriveled little woman dressed in the *traje* of my village: María Magdalena Rivas, my grandmother's friend. Tears stream down my face.

Here is someone who knew my mother who kept the fire going, my father who lifted the hoe, my grandmother who told the tales and wove the cloth.

And now I sob at my loss, and in the arms of that old, familiar woman from my village, I take comfort.

◈19◈

She reaches deep under the belt that wraps around and around her frail body and takes out a small packet, a packet worn from the journey she has made.

Inside are the sample pieces of weaving, the designs of our people. The pieces handed down by my great-great-grandmother. The ones my grandmother wanted me to have.

As I hold them in my hand, I see the brilliant colors, blue-green, gold, and red — colors of the beautiful bird from the land I love. I know then that I will not forget. I will weave our patterns, designs of light, no matter where I live. I want the world to know and remember too.

"Grandmother," I whisper, "maybe it will keep the cows on the cliffs and the sun from falling. And just maybe tonight I will ride the quetzal, my skybird to the high heavens."

Philippe and the Blue Parrot

When Philippe was a young boy, his mother told him a story about a beautiful blue parrot who stole a golden earring from the sun.

"Watch for it, Philippe, my boy," she said. "And when you find that golden earring, we will never go hungry again."

And so Philippe kept his head down as he walked to school through the streets of Port-au-Prince, always looking for a glint of gold.

Years passed. Philippe did well in his studies. He was especially good at art. When Philippe was thirteen, he decided to make a birthday gift for his mother.

He took his art supplies to the park, and there, leaning the canvas against a bench, he painted *Blue Parrot and the Sun*. As he waited for the paint to dry, he studied the blue smudges between his fingers and a drop of yellow shining on his black wrist.

"Is that for sale?"

Philippe was startled by the question. He had not heard the tourist walk up to him. The woman squinted her eyes at the bright colors and asked again.

"Is that for sale?" Before Philippe could answer, she added, "I'll pay twenty-five dollars for it."

Twenty-five dollars! That was more than Philippe had earned in his whole life. It would take a long time to make that much money, even if he could get a job. What wonderful things he could buy his mother.

And so Philippe sold *Blue Parrot and the Sun.*

Years passed. Philippe's paintings were sold in a Port-au-Prince gallery. Many tourists liked his work and bought the canvases.

Every time Philippe painted a *Blue Parrot and the Sun* for his mother, the gallery owner had a buyer. The price went up and Philippe could not resist. But every time he sold a *Blue Parrot,* he put aside some money for his mother.

Many years passed. Now Philippe's paintings could not be afforded by most tourists. His work hung in galleries and museums in Europe and the United States.

One day, he sat in his fine studio, ready to begin work on another *Blue Parrot and the Sun.* A journalist who had come to interview him stood nearby.

"Monsieur, your *Blue Parrot and the Sun* paintings are now very famous. Some critics say that they have a life and power that your other works lack. Why is that? Do you know?"

"Oh yes, I know," Philippe replied slowly. "It is because I paint each *Blue Parrot* for my mother."

"And how much will this new one sell for?" the journalist asked. "Thousands, I suppose?"

"Oh, this painting will not be for sale," Philippe answered. He knew he had said that before, but this time, he really meant it.

And he added: "I found the golden earring many years ago. Now it's time to give it back."

◆   ◆   ◆

There is a story the art collectors tell about a famous painting called *Blue Parrot and the Sun*. Oh, there are many, but the one to hunt for has a small golden earring hidden in the picture. Yes, that is the one worth a fortune. Some say it hangs on the wall of a simple house in the Haitian countryside. Others are not so sure. It could be anywhere.

The Golden Thread of Josefina Marie

Josefina Marie was born in a small village in the country-side of Haiti. Her mother, Monique Renée, had loved her well — yes, even with the first, sad words from the granny who helped bring her into the world. "Your daughter has no arms," she said.

It was a strong statement, simply put. The old woman had seen much sorrow in her long years. Perhaps her strength passed on to Monique Renée and, in turn, to Jose-fina as the old granny wiped them both off with water, cleaning them up for life.

"Let the child die," the neighbors said when they heard the news. "She will be another mouth to feed. As she grows, she will eat more rice. She will cry when her bowl is empty, but will not help to fill it. She will carry no water, pick up no wood for your fire. Let the child die!"

Monique Renée, turning her face from her neighbors, looked to the hillside where the old granny lived and said, "My child will live."

And the child did live, but never smiled.

One day, a Sister from the capital came to Josefina's village. For the first time, Josefina's mother heard that there was a school for children like her daughter. A place where she could learn to read and play with other children.

With great sadness, Monique Renée sent her Josefina Marie away with the Sister. Though it was like cutting off a piece of herself, Monique Renée did not cry. For she knew she would carry love for her child in her heart always.

Josefina Marie entered the school with a solemn face. But though the five-year-old lacked two arms, she had a quick mind. The teachers could see that she was bright and loved to learn new things.

For two years, Josefina Marie excelled in her studies. Then a volunteer came to work at the school. They called her Madame Ruth. She was old, but came to give what she could, not sure of what that would be.

She tried helping in the office, but her typing was poor. She rocked babies in the nursery, but, being a frail woman herself, found it difficult to lift them from their cribs.

One day, as she sat in the shade of the old tree that had pushed its way up through the patio, Madame Ruth pulled out a hoop of embroidery. "Madame Ruth," Sister Anne said as she hurried by on her way to the clinic. "You can teach the children to embroider!"

After lessons on Tuesday, a small group of children who wanted to learn embroidery met Madame Ruth at the east end of the patio. Josefina Marie was one of those children.

If Madame Ruth was surprised by this, she did not show it.

Instead, she calmly gave each child a wooden hoop, a needle, and some thread. Josefina Marie watched the others as they slowly began to practice the simple stitches the old woman demonstrated for them.

Madame Ruth walked over to her, bent down, and whispered into Josefina's ear: "Use what you have, my child. Use what you have." And Josefina Marie looked down at her strong, agile toes. She was already using them for writing and for feeding herself, but even so, it would take a very long time.

Whenever her lessons and chores were completed, Josefina Marie labored over her embroidery. She sat on a mat, toes poised with needle and thread, balancing the hoop against one leg. Often, she sat at Madame Ruth's feet. When she needed help, the determined old woman bent over the determined young girl. And the Sisters were amazed.

It was Josefina's idea: for Christmas, she would embroider an altar cloth of the Holy Mother and Christ Child. She was still her mother's child and the love that had helped her live those first five years burned within her.

Sometimes the Sisters worried. At first, they worried that Josefina would not succeed. She would be disappointed with the results. Later, they worried that the project had become an obsession. Sister Anne made sure that Josefina was in the proper light. Sister Margaret thought it

was not natural for a child to spend so much time in such a solitary manner. Sister Theresa was sure Josefina was getting thinner.

But Madame Ruth supplied Josefina with thread and needles and talked with no one concerning the great beauty that was taking shape. And when the cloth was finished, the old woman remained silent in her confusion. For she did not remember buying golden thread. But her reward was the light on Josefina Marie's face. And it was that light that all the Sisters would remember for many years to come.

◈   ◈   ◈

Josefina Marie's altar cloth was brought to the Cathedral on the first Sunday of Advent for the service of carols. On that same day, the deaf women who made the communion wafers heard music. Blind David who played the handbells with the choir saw a beautiful blazing star and Monique Renée, in from her country village, saw her daughter smile for the first time.

Years later, when the cloth hung behind glass and many came to see its beauty, no one recalled the name of the woman who taught Josefina Marie how to embroider. And by then, only a few knew that the golden thread of the Madonna and Child had been sewn by a young schoolgirl, making use of what she had.

Granny Vye and the Rose of Fire

Golden Wings, Samuel, Little Gem, Willy,
Tiffany, Brittany, Tanya Jo.
Wilhelmina, Tina, Birdie Blye, Blaze,
Dongada, dongada, ayeeo!

Granny Vye sang the names of her roses and the names of her "bitty babies," mixing in a little Creole from her Haiti home of long ago. She smiled, pleased with the sounds of it.

Never mind that people on this big-city bus were watching as her lips moved over the names. What did bother her was when she missed her stop and had to walk two extra blocks to Saint Luke's Hospital. Her legs were getting too old for that!

The bus stopped and Granny got off, right in front of the main entrance to Saint Luke's. For fifteen years now, she had been going through these doors and up the elevator to the third floor. Granny Vye was a volunteer in the hospital nursery, three times a week. Usually, she worked in the preemie section.

"Bitty babies born too soon. Old Granny Vye's here, just for you." That's what she said now, as she walked up to the glass and looked into the room where they lay. Each baby was enclosed in a plastic box called an isolette.

"Samuel . . . Brittany . . . Tanya Jo . . . Wilhelmina . . . Tina." Granny whispered the names like a prayer as she read the card taped to the end of each isolette. She never forgot a name.

Even after all these years, a name might come to her when she least expected it. She would smile and remember the baby face. Only a few special times had she learned of one of her "bitty babies," now grown up. Five years, seven years, thirteen years old!

"And welcome to you, Jeremiah Joshua! What a big name for a bitty baby," Granny said as she looked at the new arrival.

Granny Vye could not go into the room where these babies were hooked up to machines. But there were other things she could do.

She brought candy to give to the big brother or sister she might find looking wide-eyed through the nursery window. She tidied the waiting room, where she kept a big vase of her beautiful roses. When a frightened new mother needed to talk, Granny Vye listened. And by the end of the day, the roses were gone. Each went home with a mother or father whose baby stayed behind.

"Elisha John, you're not alone, sweet pumpkin. Granny

Vye is here," she crooned softly as she walked into the room where one baby lay in an uncovered crib.

Elisha John was out of the intensive-care nursery. Now he was ready to go home, but there was no home. There was no family waiting for him. He was the one Granny could hold in her arms and rock. He was the one who needed her most.

By the end of the day, Granny climbed back on the bus and went home, smelling like roses and babies. Their names were still on her lips.

Golden Wings, Samuel, Little Gem, Willy,
Tiffany, Brittany, Tanya Jo.
Wilhelmina, Tina, Birdie Blye, Blaze,
Dongada, dongada, ayeeo!

On Saturday morning, Granny sat weeding in her small garden. She leaned back on an old, green pillow and rested. Her knobby knees throbbed and her back ached from bending over.

She had her Christmas-box project to work on when she took a break from weeding. A shoe box and a few old Christmas cards were spread out on the grass beside her. Granny looked at the cards now. Her eyes stopped at a picture of the Holy Family. She pulled a small pair of scissors from her apron pocket and carefully cut around the mother, father, and baby.

"Every bitty baby needs a family," she murmured. "No matter what."

Granny reached into her other pocket and pulled out a small white bottle of glue. She carefully pasted the picture to the top of the box. This would hold her Christmas money for the babies. It was not too early to start saving. Granny smiled as she shook the box with the $5.26 she had put in that morning.

She placed the box beside her favorite climbing rose — a huge bush that grew almost eight feet up the trellis. This plant was called Blaze and made her think of the story of Moses and the Burning Bush in the Bible.

Granny turned back to her weeding and did not look up again until she heard a loud voice. A teenage boy pushed his way, cursing, into her yard.

"Hey, old woman!" he yelled. "I need money. Give me what you have or you'll be sorry."

Granny was already sorry. Sorry for his crude ways, sorry for his mama. She thought of the hospital and Elisha John and his new, fresh life. She thought of his family who did not want him. She thought of the fuzzy stuffed dog she wanted to buy him for Christmas.

"What's this, old woman?"

The boy grabbed for the box. But as he reached for it, his fingers brushed a petal on the rosebush. Or was it a thorn?

He dropped the box as if it were hot. As if he had

touched fire. Fire from the rose named Blaze. He knelt there in the grass and did not say a word.

Granny Vye studied his face and whispered, "Sweet rose of Sharon! Tyrone." And she reached out her hand to him. The confused boy ignored the old woman's outstretched hand, but he could not lower his eyes. In them flickered a small remembering.

Getting up, he awkwardly pulled out some crumpled dollar bills from his back pocket and stuffed them into Granny Vye's box. Then he ran out of the yard without looking back.

Granny Vye slowly stood and lifted both arms to the sky. "God be praised!" she shouted, and then added: "Where there's fire, there's light. Send that boy straight to his mama!"

On Monday morning, as Granny Vye rode the bus that took her to the "bitty babies," she chanted:

> *Golden Wings, Samuel, Little Gem, Willy,*
> *Tiffany, Brittany, Tanya Jo.*
> *Wilhelmina, Tina, Birdie Blye, Blaze,*
> *Tyrone, dongada, ayeeo!*

Federico's *Fantástico* Day

Clickity-click. Clickity-click. The end of the stick Federico was holding in his hand hit the chain link fence. It sang out a rhythm that Federico liked. He felt good. *¡Muy bien!*

Suddenly, Federico wanted to run. Run and jump and dance. Funny how a little sound could make you feel *fantástico*. Even in this big city of New York, where noise usually drowned out the small sounds.

And yet, Federico knew it was really more than the sound of the stick on the fence. There was also the bowl of warm cereal that had filled his stomach this cold morning, and Mamá's new job, and the way his little sister Bettina's round, brown eyes looked up at him.

Federico gripped the stick tightly and slowly limped to school. Last summer, he had felt a similar burst of happiness. It was the day the big kids asked him to play ball. He tried hard to show them how good he was. Catching the ball was all he cared about as he ran out into the busy street.

The next thing he remembered was the bright, white light of the hospital. And the doctor's name. Dr. Apple! He wanted to laugh when he heard that name, but it hurt too much. *¡Muy malo!*

Then there were the long days and nights in bed. First in the hospital, then at home. Tía Rosa had come to stay with him while Mamá worked at the factory.

Federico remembered how surprised he had been the first time he tried to pick up a schoolbook. How could something as little as that seem so heavy?

Now he could walk and carry his schoolbooks. And he could grip this stick in his hand. This singing stick. But to run and jump and dance . . . and shoot a basket! Would he ever?

Mr. Jackson, the gym teacher, believed he would. He had said so. And he had loaned Federico the bottle-shaped clubs. "Throw these every day after school and your arms will grow strong again," Mr. Jackson had told him.

So every day after school, Federico threw the old, white, wooden clubs with the band of blue around the bottom. He threw them in the little yard outside the apartment and marked his progress by where they landed.

Over and over again, Federico lifted his arm and threw. He could hear the clumping sound the clubs made as they hit the ground, even in his sleep. But it was a good sound and never woke him up.

As Federico turned in at the old, redbrick building,

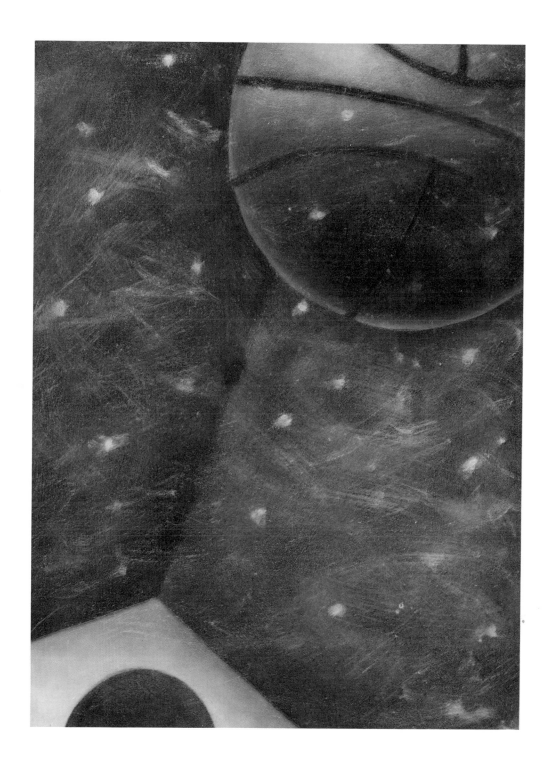

small flakes of snow began to fall. He stuck out his tongue
to catch them. They were like tiny falling stars.

Suddenly, Federico thought of Sister Elma. She was the
neighbor who lived in the apartment next to his. Sometimes her loud singing voice came right through the walls.
Today, Sister Elma woke him with "My Lord, what a morning. My Lord, what a morning. My Lord, what a morning
when the stars begin to fall."

Gym class was in the afternoon. By that time, you could
hear the students' excitement in the noisy echoes that
filled the halls. Snow was still falling and everyone said
school would get out early.

At one-thirty, Federico knelt down, carefully tightened
the laces on his sneakers, and then got in line to wait for
Mr. Jackson. He came soon, carrying the beloved basket-
ball. Federico shivered with anticipation. Maybe today!

The class took turns shooting baskets in the dreary, gray
gym. Federico looked up and could barely see the falling
snow in the dim light of the barred windows.

Then it was his turn. "My Lord, what a morning," he
hummed as he lifted both arms. Then he pushed. Up, up,
up the ball went, as if into a swirling sky of falling, white
stars. Federico grinned.

Back in the classroom, Mrs. Flores told them to get out
their math workbooks. All of a sudden, Dana jumped up
out of his seat.

"Teacher! Teacher!" he shouted. "Federico made a

basket!" And then all twenty-nine second-graders jumped to their feet, clapping and cheering. "Federico made a basket! Federico made a basket!"

Federico smiled at his classmates. He smiled at his teacher. He smiled as the bell rang. He walked out of school into the swirling snow. And the light on his face and the joy in his heart kept him warm all the way home.

◈   ◈

Author's Note

Although I have visited the areas where these stories are set, only "Federico's *Fantástico* Day" was based on an actual event. I was the teacher in that story.

There really was a student in my class who had been hit by a car. The gym teacher worked with the boy as he tried very hard to regain the normal use of his arms and legs. And there really were twenty-nine students who spontaneously applauded him because he had shot a basket in gym class. That was many years ago. I have never forgotten that small kindness.

I wrote these stories to help him remember, and also because of an experience I had in a tiny village in Mexico. It happened long ago too. If I could write a letter to the people there, this is what I would say:

I was a stranger. I visited your village. You welcomed me. You brought a chair for me to sit on. You fixed food for me to eat. You drew water from the well so that I could wash.

◈ 41 ◈

◈LIGHT◈

When it was time for me to leave, you shook my hand. You smiled and gave me an egg, blazing white in the full, fierce sun.

As I rode the bus that took me out of your village, the egg broke. I was sorry. Not because the broken egg smelled in the heat of the day, or felt sticky on the palm of my hand, or stained my clothing. I was sorry because I had been careless with your fragile gift.

Since that time, I have been more careful with a small kindness.